THE HOLE

A Fable that takes you on a Journey
Through the Struggle with Emptiness
in your Life

By
Bruce Derman, Ph.D.

23011 Oxnard St
Woodland Hills, California 91367
818-375-7194
RelationDr@aol.com
web site: therelationshipdoctor.net

ISBN: 1450540678
ISBN-13: 9781450540674

DEDICATION

This book is dedicated to my grandsons Gavin and Cayden, who are just beginning their life journeys. My hope is that they will be able to use the wisdom of this story to guide them through their lives.

ACKNOWLEDGEMENTS

There are numerous people who have supported me in working and reworking this book over the years it has taken me to complete it. I especially want to thank Michael Hauge, who has written two books himself, for being there from the beginning and always being an honest and articulate voice. I want to express my deepest appreciation to my wife, Marla, for supporting me emotionally and mentally through this process and being a constant sounding board. I also want to thank my sister, Susan Cole, my step son Matt Gorlick, as well as William Atherton, Judy Morris, Shelley Pearce, and Barbara and Dan Aranda for their time and contributions. A final thank you to my editor, Ruth, for her detailed work in making this difficult material cohesive.

TABLE OF CONTENTS

Chapter		Page

INTRODUCTION ⚭

Many of us walk down our respective life roads and eventually get exposed to a door that says on it, in big letters, ENTRANCE TO NOTHING. This traumatic event may have been caused by a job loss, financial setback, death, or the ending of a relationship. Regardless of the trigger, we feel sadness, emptiness, and the very real possibility that we will lose the life we thought we had and the sense of who we thought we were. As a result, we fail to see anything positive about stepping out through this apparent doorway to nothing, which, in our minds would expose us to our fears of becoming nothing. Instead, we attempt to flee through whatever means possible. Some of us believe we are successful in escaping, others try not to care, and a few will deny that this door even exists. Regardless of the method used, it is intended to stamp out the threat of this feeling that we are nothing.

Due to these negative perceptions of nothingness it is rare that any of us are open to the benefits and secrets that lie beyond this door. One of the secrets is that we can discover our real truths and passions only by entering this door. If we avoid or ignore the door, or deny its very existence, we will be compelled to find ways to merely cope with our lives, to adapt to unpleasant circumstances, and to survive. But we will not thrive. We will not find our true destiny. The second secret benefit is that only by going through this door can we get off the treadmill of pursuing insatiable goals and instead find inner contentment. The last secret is that this doorway to nothing can put us on the path to new beginnings. By stepping through it, we will discover this paradox: only by letting go of the ego attachments that we cling to in our life and allowing the experience of nothing are we able to open ourselves to new experiences in our life. In the end, only those of us who are willing to walk through this door and learn to accept the emptiness we dread are able to experience the depth of who we really are. By respecting the process of moving through this door, we are able to see that emptiness is not an end but is, in fact, a beginning to a truly rich, internal life where we can manifest our true expressive nature.

To be sure, this can be a daunting process. By walking through this door we will encounter our greatest fear: the unknown. Looking into the unknown and its dark recesses is especially scary to all of us. This intense fear often seems unbearable to many of us, especially when we come face to face with what seems like an unending emptiness. Emptiness is defined as the void we experience in our lives whenever we leave any part of our familiar world and embark on a new direction, even though that new path has yet to emerge. It can be as simple as moving from talking with a group of people to a moment of awkward silence; or it can be as profound as a career change.

It is little wonder, then, that we desperately try to find ways to protect, deny, or hide ourselves from this empty feeling. Some of us choose to be strong or perfect, while others prefer to be pleasing. Many people would rather abuse drugs or alcohol, or become workaholics, or embrace any other addiction rather than encounter feelings of emptiness. The overall thinking is that experiencing *something* has got to be better than experiencing *nothing*. Despite these attempts, the dreaded feeling of emptiness continues to emerge and re-emerge in many areas of our lives. The challenge of what to do with our emptiness is shared by all of us. In the spirit of that ongoing struggle, and with the hope of helping people to make peace with their greatest fear, I share this story.

I must caution you that the concepts contained in this story may be seen as more abstract than most books you have read. If this is the case, I recommend that you expand the capacity of your openness by letting go of the thinking and conditioning that you are most familiar with. It also may be helpful if you allowed yourself to *think* stoned in contrast to *being* stoned.

Bruce Derman, Ph.D.

CHAPTER ONE ❧

A HOLE WITHIN

Once upon a time in a land similar to the one we all know, a young married couple named Dawn and Dirk lived happily together in a lovely new home in the suburbs. To their friends and neighbors their relationship appeared idyllic – a dream come true. Although seldom apart, they never tired of each other's company and all who knew them regarded them as a perfect couple.

Even physically they reflected an impressive image. Dirk would always be seen as clean shaven with an immaculate hair style, and with a body to match because he worked out at the gym five times a week. Not to be outdone, Dawn was a Barbie look-alike with long flowing blonde hair, perfectly manicured nails, and of course, her make-up was never out of place.

Gratified by their image, our young couple believed they had the key to a happy and fulfilling relationship. Dawn and Dirk had all the material trappings of the good life — a new car for each of them every two or three years, the latest appliances, flat screen TVs the size of picture windows, and powerful computers with lightning fast Internet service. They were always dressed in the latest and most expensive fashions. What's more, their house was a show-piece: expensively yet tastefully furnished with beautiful hardwood floors. The cost of all these comforts was easily managed since both of them had highly paid careers; he as head of his own advertising agency and she as direc-tor of public relations for a multinational corporation.

Of course, there were some people, motivated perhaps by envy, who suspected that this image of per-fection was merely a façade. However, none of these doubters were able to dent the image of harmonious perfection that this couple displayed. Even if it were merely an act, both Dawn and Dirk totally believed it. In fact, their public personas mirrored their life behind closed doors; they virtually never clashed. Unlike most typical relationships, in which a particular role or attri-bute is used by one partner to create an inflated sense of self leading to antagonism or resentment in the other, theirs was a partnership in which both of them regarded the other as flawless and saw their match as perfect.

Even their friends, who wished them well, couldn't help feeling envious when encountering a couple that always appeared to be so genuinely happy and suc-cessful together. Quite often, Dawn or Dirk would be conscripted into another couple's marital quarrel. "Why can't you be successful like Dirk?" a discontented wife might ask her struggling husband. And he might reply in kind, "Why can't you be there for me as Dawn is for Dirk?" When friends shared their frustrations with Dawn and Dirk, the perfect couple would urge them not to make such comparisons. Always gracious and thoughtful, they didn't wish to be the cause of ill feelings; but inwardly they were gratified by a sense of their superiority.

Dirk frequently commented to Dawn about the many problems that impaired the relationships of their family and friends. He was amazed that other people were unable to live the happy life they enjoyed. Like Dirk, Dawn couldn't imagine living any other way than they did, and she believed that their way of life was an ideal to be emulated by any couple in quest of an intimate relationship.

As you might imagine, this wasn't the whole story. In time, this beautiful picture would start to crack, but only through very unusual circumstances.

While Dawn always maintained an air of contentment and agreement, she was secretly troubled by feelings and thoughts that she didn't dare share with Dirk for fear of displeasing him. While their life did seem wonderful on the surface, deep within herself she harbored doubts, uneasiness, and a strange sense of emptiness. Could it be that their intimacy was too perfect and had become somehow mechanical? There were moments when she found herself wanting to scream and behave like an irre-sponsible idiot in order to break out of the confinement of their perfectly manicured existence. She wondered if she was neglecting some inherent need inside herself, but she couldn't put her finger on it. All of these thoughts created an uncomfortable dissonance within her and produced guilty feelings for even having these thoughts in the face of their "wonderful" existence. In the end she just tried to wipe these thoughts and feelings away by ignoring them. This worked until . . .

One day a mysterious thing happened that turned their happy world upside down. It was something so small at first that it was hard to believe it could end up having such a devastating effect.

A tiny hole appeared in the middle of their living room, piercing the beautifully finished cherry wood floor.

At first only Dawn knew about it. She noticed a little mark – somewhat bigger than the size of a pin head – that a person with a less attentive eye probably wouldn't have seen. To Dawn it was not only there, it was a constant annoyance. Her biggest concern, of course, was that Dirk would see this blemish and that it would greatly displease him, so she kept it from him as best she could.

In the ensuing weeks she tried to fill the pinhole with putty that matched the floor, and anything else she could find in the store, but none of it had any effect for reasons she just couldn't fathom. She struggled to contain her increasing frustration over this hole in their perfection, afraid that Dirk would notice.

On one particular day, when Dirk and Dawn were enjoying a game together and were seemingly oblivious to anything but each other, she could contain her concern no longer. Unable to pretend that there was nothing amiss, Dawn suddenly exclaimed, "Look over there."

Dirk was startled and wondered why she was so excited. "It's probably nothing," he told himself. "That's just how women are."

But he turned and reacted viscerally as she pointed and screamed, "Over there, over there!"

Then he saw what she was pointing to. In the middle of the hardwood floor in their living room was a small hole. It was perhaps no more than a half inch in diameter, but it was definitely a hole where you wouldn't expect one to be. Dawn was even more alarmed because she already knew that the hole, while still small, was definitely bigger than the mere pockmark she had noticed a few weeks ago.

"Maybe we're just seeing things," Dirk quickly noted. "After all, people have messes in their houses, not holes, and we don't even have disarray." Either way, a mess or a hole in their house was unthinkable to him. So he looked again, willing it to disappear, but it was still there. Not comfortable without answers, Dirk began to search for a cause he could understand. "Could there have been an earthquake and we didn't notice it?" he wondered, without asking himself how an earthquake could produce a round hole in the middle of his living room floor; a hole through the polished cherry wood that did not looked drilled but seemed organic, almost as if caused by disease. Holding desperately on to his initial thought, he insisted that they turn on the news, but none of the TV channels reported an earthquake or any similar event. In pursuit of a rational explanation, Dirk asked, "Do you know if anyone poked something into the floor by mistake?"

Dawn shook her head. "No, I didn't see anyone do that."

"What about the housekeeper?" he asked, trying every avenue he could think of. "She's had accidents in the past."

"She would have told me if something happened."

"Maybe we just didn't notice it before," Dirk said, wondering if the hole had been there when they bought the house.

"I spotted it three weeks ago," Dawn confessed. "But I was afraid to say anything. It's disturbed me every time we came in here. How could *you* have missed it?" she asked him incredulously.

"True, it's not like me to miss noticing things, but I'm embarrassed to admit that I really did miss this one."

Acknowledging the hole's existence didn't explain how it came to be there or even how deep it might be. Gingerly they stood up and moved closer to the hole and peeked inside, but they could see nothing. "How far down does it go?" Dawn asked.

Dirk got a ten-foot wire out of the garage, which the gardeners had left. He stuck it into the hole – three feet, then five feet, and still he felt no bottom. Then he stuck it in a full ten feet, but it didn't make a difference. There seemed to be no bottom to this hole. They were both bewildered by this since their home was only one story high with no basement. Dawn, clearly feeling uneasy about not knowing the depth of the hole, dashed outside and grabbed a small stone from the footpath and threw it into the hole's opening. Seconds went by, but they heard no sound. They waited another minute: still nothing. It was obvious that not only did they have an ugly hole in their living room floor, but also it was a seemingly bottomless hole, an empty space, a total void, a deep something with nothing in it.

Bottomless or not, this disfigurement had a great impact on their otherwise perfect home: it had created an imperfection. Encountering this palpable flaw, the couple felt their happiness and peace began to be undermined by anxiety and suspicion. Dawn worried that Dirk would never be content living in a defective house. She feared that it would disrupt their relationship. Dirk, on the other hand, was struggling for answers and searching for someone to blame for the flaw. "What had caused the hole? Whose fault was it? Why should this even happen to us?" he wondered, but kept these thoughts to himself.

They both pondered relentlessly on how they might get rid of it. They wondered who they could call to take care of it. They looked in the Yellow Pages for hole removers – there were none. They looked again for hole fixers and found a contractor who claimed he could fix any and all unwanted holes. They hired him, and when he arrived he poured concrete into the hole, which by this time had grown to six inches. Then he put in new wood boards perfectly fitted to cover the opening. Dirk and Dawn gladly paid him and thanked him for his help. They assumed that their troubles were over and that the house was back intact again. But no sooner was the contractor gone than the hole mysteriously came back – in the exact same spot and it was as big as ever.

Their attention shifted momentarily from the hole as they contemplated calling the contractor back and expressing their dissatisfaction with his work. What if someone found out that there was this awful opening in the middle of their perfect house? This last question became their most urgent focus.

Each, in turn, thought how terrible it would be for anyone else to see how this problem disfigured their pristine image. They were afraid that if people knew about this imperfection, they would be the talk of the neighborhood – and not in a good way. The thought occurred to them that their neighbors might wonder that if Dawn and Dirk had one imperfection, maybe they had others! The threat of that made them very uneasy. They tried to reassure each other.

"Maybe it will just go away," said Dawn hopefully. "After all, it just appeared out of nowhere.

"Maybe," Dirk replied doubtfully.

Mesmerized by the hole, they sat and stared at it for several hours, wishing that it would vanish. But it did not disappear. Tense with anxiety, Dawn finally spoke.

"Tomorrow we have company coming over. Can't you do something right away to fix this problem?"

Dirk tried to calm her and suggested that they put a rug over it and place a table on top of that. She agreed and it seemed to work. The next day they anxiously watched their guests as they arrived, but no one seemed to notice that the rug and table were hiding anything.

For the next few months they were able to generally ignore the hole. But one evening Dirk's curiosity got the better of him. He wanted to see if the hole was actually still there. Dawn was a little apprehensive about finding out, but as usual she went along with Dirk's desire. They found their flashlights and slowly lifted the rug. To their astonishment, they saw that the hole had gotten larger. It was now a foot wide and still seemed bottomless as they shone their flashlights into its depths.

The hole continued to expand over the ensuing weeks, and as it grew, so did their fear that someone would find out. In an effort to avoid the embarrassment of that occurring, whenever anyone came over, they always had it covered with bigger rugs and larger pieces of furniture.

"Why do you keep changing the furniture in your living room?" a friend asked quizzically. "We just like a lot of variety in our home," was one of Dirk and Dawn's pre-arranged replies, as they made eye contact over their shared secret.

Consequently, Dirk and Dawn soon found themselves in an endlessly repeating scenario. The hole was now widening into a sizable pit, and covering it required larger and larger rugs underneath whatever tables they chose. The ever-expanding hole sucked each new rug through its opening. The carpet dealers they patronized were gratified to receive so much business, but were equally puzzled wondering why this couple needed to replace such well-made expensive rugs so frequently.

The couple lived in a constant state of fear, terrified that sooner or later their secret would be discovered. They were fairly sure that none of the other couples they knew had such an unsightly hole in their homes. So if someone brought up decorating, furniture, or any other subject that was even remotely related to their coverup, they quickly and clearly changed the topic.

"I see you have new rugs," asked a neighbor.

"Yes, and I see you have a new dog. Tell us about him. Is he pedigree?"

In their town, Dirk and Dawn became known as the couple who always had great, new rugs and imaginative new furniture arrangements, which was a far better image than being talked about as the couple who had a big, ugly, empty hole in the middle of their home. The threat of the widening void became in interminable struggle for them. Every day and every night they were consumed with finding some way to get rid of the hole. It occupied their every waking moment. They were constantly asking each other, "What will it take to fill the hole?" Neither knew the answer.

To live with such an ugly hole and the obsessive awareness that it was getting bigger and bigger, made the couple's previous happiness a distant memory. Dawn's initial concern about their existence being too manicured was certainly not even an issue these days.

By now the hole had grown into a chasm several feet across. Even as they sought to hide it from their neighbors it continued to grow, defying their efforts to diminish it. If Dirk and Dawn tried to resist its growth, it would expand an additional inch: hide it – another inch; seek ways to eliminate it – another inch. Responding to their unending rejection, it relentlessly grew wider and wider and indeed became overwhelming within a relatively short time. But even by this stage, they were totally unaware that the hole was growing in response to their efforts to contain it.

So the painful process continued year after year. As a couple and as individuals, Dawn and Dirk sought ways to fill the increasing huge void in their home.

As the hole widened, they found that hiding it with rugs and furniture was impossible and they had to resort to more extreme measures. On the advice of a new contractor, they brought in truckloads of dirt in an attempt to fill the hole rather than just cover it up. But since the hole was bottomless, this turned out to be just as futile as the earlier concrete.

Trying to explain to their neighbors why all this dirt was being hauled inside their home, they came up with some ludicrous excuses such as, "It's the new look this year," or "We are considering a rustic décor." However, even as they tried to explain away their intentions with the dirt, it continued to rapidly disappear into the ever-deepening hole . The hole stayed just as empty as before.

Since the dirt didn't work, they decided to try water. In a moment of pure inspiration, Dawn excitedly said, "Let's turn the hole into an indoor swimming pool so we can get some enjoyment out of it!" But no matter how much water they put in, the hole drained it and remained empty.

Then they decided to try stuffing numerous strips of ceiling insulation into the hole, since it was designed to fill empty spaces. Initially they were excited and hopeful that this might work, but again, just like the contractor's dirt, the insulation failed them.

Undeterred by these failures, they persisted in their efforts to conquer the hole. And there were heady moments when they believed they had succeeded. "At last, I have found the answer!" Dirk announced one day, confident in spite of all their past failures. He found a rubber material that would inflate to any size and stick to the side of any surface. He quickly inflated it, placed it in the hole, and for a moment things looked promising.

"The hole is filled! We've done it! No more big, empty hole!"

Dawn rejoiced with him, but their elation was short lived. As with all their previous efforts, this one was doomed to failure. The stickiness slipped off and the rubber material was swallowed by the ever-expanding hole. Once again the hole remained empty, gaping rebelliously before them.

After so many failures, Dirk was becoming increasingly pessimistic and discouraged. Dawn tried to encourage him, still hoping that they might recover their lost happiness, but eventually she, too, became discouraged and shared her husband's doubts that they would ever find a solution. Nothing, it seemed, would ever fill this void.

Unanswerable questions continued to bombard their thoughts. "How did this happen to us? How does this hole devour everything we put into it? Is there some kind of powerful suction force under the house? Is the hole actually the gaping maw of some alien being able to swallow anything? Perhaps the whole nightmare is part of a new show that combines Candid Camera with the Twilight Zone?" They just wished the show would end and that someone would say, "Smile, you're on the Candid Zone."

Unable to find a workable solution, they attempted to ignore the problem altogether, hoping it might go away. While the frightening emptiness still dominated their home and defied their efforts to fill it, they could manage to turn away and tell themselves that they didn't need to deal with it. This being decided, they would find any excuse to get out of the house – it didn't matter where – just so they wouldn't have to be at home. However, they soon found out that a play or a movie could only provide a temporary diversion. They always had to return to the house and all the frustrations they sought to evade.

Still hoping to escape, they became workaholics, and when they weren't working, they were busy acquiring new things. Hardly a week passed without some new acquisition – a car, a painting, a boat. The pressure of debt that came with all this buying was offset, to some extent, by the temporary rush of excitement that enabled them to forget about the hole. But the pleasure of acquiring a new possession was fleeting, while the credit card debt remained and grew – much like the hole – and soon their momentary exhilaration would give way to depression.

Next, they tried switching to less costly distractions. Dirk would immerse himself in television and play for hours on the Internet, while Dawn went through book after book. Thus, they would continuously divert themselves, but still they couldn't escape the reality of the hole's continued existence. Try as they might to deny it, the hole remained and continued to grow inexorably.

And the effects of living with it – exhaustion, frustration, anger, and sadness – began to show in their faces, mirroring the confirmation of their worst fear: that the hole would be with them forever.

CHAPTER TWO ❧

LIVING WITH THE HOLE

Four years passed, and they still strove to maintain their appearance of perfection and tried to please each other in the process. But after four years of living with the hole and trying to contain it, it was becoming more difficult to maintain their image or to make the effort to please each other. Perpetually on the edge of their respective comfort zone, they sank into doubt and lost their shared optimistic outlook. Their nerves and bodies were tense with anxiety, and they began to vent it in mutual recrimination.

It began with gentle teasing and a little gallows humor to relieve the tension. Dirk told his wife that he was thinking about putting her into the opening as a human sacrifice to appease the gods who ruled over the hole. Perhaps she could make herself useful as an acceptable sacrifice.

"Very funny," Dawn replied. "You are such a big KNOW IT ALL, why can't you come up with a real solution to our problem? That would be something useful."

Then they would engage in caustic banter, some of which was gender focused.

"When a woman marries someone, she always hopes that she can turn him into the man she really wants. But you haven't changed," Dawn provoked.

"When a man marries someone, he always hopes that she won't change, but you certainly have," Dirk retaliated.

"You are living proof that a woman can take a joke."

"I can get past my mistakes. Why can't you?"

And so it went on. Pretty soon the banter became more cutting and there were accusations.

"You should have noticed this hole when we picked this house," Dawn muttered, just loud enough for Dirk to hear. Then she would speak up and hit him below the belt. "You're a man and you should know how to fix things. It's a man's responsibility to deal with a hole in his house."

Then just as they seemed to be losing all sense of happiness, they were blessed by an event that seemed to turn things around. Dawn became pregnant. They were joyfully anticipating the arrival, and when a beautiful baby girl was delivered, their delight knew no bounds. They named her Beatrice Ann after Dirk's mother. This new love filled their home, and not only did the hole no longer matter, but it even seemed to be shrinking. It appeared by creating life, they had found a way to fill it. Why hadn't they thought about this idea before so they could have had the baby sooner?

Yet even this perfect solution to their problem was destined to fail. As life with the baby became part of their normal routine, the hole grew wider again. The baby grew into a toddler. Fearing that she might fall into the hole, they had a collapsible toddler fence designed to stretch around its circumference. But there was no containing the fact that they had been defeated again.

Toward the end of her pregnancy Dawn decided to give up her career in public relations and become a fulltime homemaker and mother. And Dirk, now under additional pressure as the only breadwinner, was resentful and couldn't understand why she would even think about blaming him for the hole. He considered the home now to be her job to take care of and clean. After all, he went off every day and took on extra assignments just to pay for their home with a hole in it. Now the housekeeper wanted extra pay for working around it, and he had to bring in contractors and plumbers! If she was going to stay at home, he figured, the least she could do was find some way to take care of the place.

Soon each was placing the blame entirely on the other, both prompted by a sense of righteous conviction.

"It's your fault this stupid hole is still here!" accused Dawn, her conviction supported by a book title she'd heard called *We'd Have a Great Relationship if it Weren't for You*, and the more they fought and dumped on each other, the faster the hole seemed to grow.

Quite often one of them would be so consumed with guilt for being mean to the other, that he or she would then reverse course and take all the blame for the hole. But that didn't help either because the hole grew just as fast when they blamed themselves as when they condemned each other.

There were moments during their intense bitter exchanges when they actually forgot about the cause of their quarrelling: the hole itself. This on its own might have been a relief, but the hole just kept on growing even as they raged. Of course, no one can rage twenty-four hours a day, but when the storm of recrimination finally passed, the hole remained for all to see, just as big and unsightly as ever.

The hole had become the center of their lives whether they were quarrelling about it or seeking a solution for it. It preoccupied them entirely. Yet they dared not give up trying to deal with it because to do so would mean abandoning any hope of recovering their happy existence. Still, in spite of their efforts they steadily began to sink into despair. Dirk's inability to control the hole disheartened him making him unable to maintain the ideal image he had of himself as the strong man of the house, while Dawn was equally crushed to see her image as a pleasant and giving person crumble and be replaced by an irritable shrew.

After the major disappointment that the baby didn't solve their problems, allowing themselves to hope at all anymore was too painful. All they could do was lament their predicament, but their feeble voices became weaker and weaker. "If only we could find that special something to fill it … If only we could find that special … If only we could …"

Finally the tension became so great on one particular day that they just exploded at each other inflicting deep, hurtful wounds.

Dawn raged at Dirk, "I hate you and I wish I'd never married you!"

Dirk retorted, "I'd certainly be better off without a woman like you!"

Each felt how unbearably painful it was to hear that this person that they loved could be so hurtful. Equally painful was the realization that they were inflicting the same pain on each other.

Dawn began to cry uncontrollably. "I'm sorry," she said. "I can't stand hurting you. I miss how it used to be."

Hearing the depth of sadness in her voice and seeing the extent of her vulnerability, Dirk broke down and said, "I'm deeply sorry too, Dawn, for the way I've treated you. I don't want to hurt you anymore."

They shared a deep intimacy as they allowed themselves to be touched by the experience. Tears flowed down both of their faces, and they longed for the days past and the love they once knew. Dirk put his arms around her, and she sobbed against his chest. For several moments neither spoke. Then Dawn raised her head and looked into her husband's face. The same thought had come to both of them, that neither of them was alone.

CHAPTER THREE ᦔᦸ

THE "HOLY" GUIDE

No one had come into the house, but when Dawn looked over Dirk's shoulder at the open window she saw the top of a stovepipe hat.

"There's someone out there!" she said, startled, nodding toward the window.

Turning, Dirk saw the hat, too. Then there was a knock at the door. When Dirk opened it he found a little man barely three feet tall on the doorstep. He was rather sloppily dressed and emitted a strange, unpleasant odor. Dirk whispered disdainfully to Dawn, "We must have expanded the criteria for our A list."

Pretending not to hear that comment, the little man said, "I heard your cry for help." The couple looked at each other wondering how on earth they could have summoned such a person. The little man continued, "I heard about your struggle with the hole in your home."

Somewhat taken aback, Dirk inquired, "How could that be since we haven't told anyone? Did our neighbors say anything to you?"

The little man, seeing the couple becoming more and more suspicious, answered quickly. "No, no one has said anything."

"Then how could you know about the hole?"

"Everyone has one," he replied.

This astonished them. "No one ever said anything to us!" exclaimed Dawn.

"So what else is new," the little man responded matter-of-factly, and decided to play with them. "Why are you so surprised? Are you sure that you never told anyone?"

"No, of course not."

"Then why would you think that they'd tell you?"

Having been so consumed with their struggle, they hadn't ever considered that possibility, but it made a lot of sense.

"I guess you're right," Dirk responded. "They would probably be as frightened and embarrassed as we are."

With that the little man invited himself in and walked casually over to the hole, which now was ten feet wide and sat down dangling his feet over the edge. Dirk and Dawn were amazed how relaxed this small fellow was around the hole that frightened them. He showed absolutely no fear of falling into the bottomless void. They ventured closer to the edge where he was sitting, yet maintained a comfortable distance. It was much too scary to get near it these days because of its sheer size. They had long since stopped having people over because they couldn't cover it anymore.

Dawn asked the little man, "Aren't you scared to be near it?"

"No, should I be?"

"Well, of course. It's a bottomless hole, which you could fall into and never come out alive."

"How do you know that?"

Dirk and Dawn were aghast at being asked such a ridiculous question. "We just know that," Dirk replied.

Unfazed, the little man retorted, "Based on what experience? Have you ever gone into the hole?"

"Of course not! We're trying to get rid of it, not go into it. We just try to be careful not to fall in."

"What a shameful waste of time," responded the little man.

"What in the world do you mean?" Dirk snapped.

"It's too soon to answer that; you wouldn't understand now."

While they hardly understood much of what the little man was saying, they felt a great sense of relief that they could finally talk to someone who knew about holes. Throughout all the years since it had appeared, they hadn't dared to talk to anyone about it except each other, fearing that people would make fun of them – or worse. Longing to trust and to be open with another person about their secret, they willingly admitted their embarrassment and fear to him. He listened with what appeared to be mild interest.

Impatiently, Dirk asked the inevitable questions, the ones that nagged them constantly. "Well, what do you do with it? How do you get rid of it?"

In a matter-of-fact tone he said, "You don't."

Their faces fell. "We were hoping you could tell us what to do," said Dawn in a desperate voice.

"I can," answered the little man.

"But you just said that we can't get rid of it. That was no solution."

"No, it simply isn't the one you want to hear. I can help you, but I am not sure you are ready to trust me and do as I say."

Dirk was thinking, "Trust you? We can barely stand the sight of you. You're NOT really the kind of person that we typically look up to, let alone depend on for something this crucial," but decided to keep this to himself.

I understand that I'm not packaged the way you desire a teacher to be. It's up to you."

"How did you know I was thinking that?" Dirk asked, slightly embarrassed.

The little man ignored the question, but said, "You're welcome to wait for someone to come along who is more to your taste."

Having nowhere else to turn and having exhausted every resource, Dirk and Dawn felt they had no choice but to trust the little man despite his unappealing appearance and manner.

Seeing that they weren't quite ready to listen to him and do as he said, he gave them other options to consider. "You could move somewhere else." But then he added, "Of course there won't be much point because there is going to be a hole wherever you go."

At first the couple disagreed with this assumption, as well as how the little man could possibly know such a thing. Still, it aroused their curiosity and they wondered if what he said about their neighbors is true.

"How have the others gotten rid of theirs?" Dawn asked.

He smiled and replied, "I don't recall saying that any of them had."

"Well then, what did they do?" Dirk wanted to know.

"Many have tried to move or have attempted a variety of the solutions you have already experimented with, and had the same level of success as you, I might add. In your favor, some of them are able to pretend that they are more successful than they are. I've always appreciated your honesty. When you failed, you didn't fake it."

Clearly intrigued, Dirk asked, "Are you saying that you've been watching us all this time? We never saw you before today."

"True. You can't see me until you reach a certain point of availability and openness. I've knocked on your door before, but you never heard me so you never answered."

"That's impossible. We never have trouble hearing someone knocking."

"Perhaps you were so distracted with other things that you were not able to hear me."

Dirk was unconvinced, but he was curious about what the little man might propose. "Well, besides moving, what else can you tell us to do? We definitely can't go on like this anymore."

"You could try something that you haven't done yet, which has worked for a lot of couples."

"What is that? Please tell us."

"You won't like it."

"Stop teasing. We're open to anything."

"Well then, here it is: you can split up. Then you wouldn't have to keep blaming each other for the empty bottomless hole and you could each marry someone else."

The couple looked at him sadly and shook their heads. He was right; this certainly was an option that they didn't want to consider. The thought of being without each other, leaving behind all of their memories and starting over was unbearable. It was terrifying to hear even the suggestion.

"We don't want to do that!" they replied simultaneously.

"We love each other too much," Dawn said tearfully. "Dirk is the only man who ever touched my heart."

"I don't want any other woman," Dirk insisted.

The little man nodded. "I suspected that would be your reply. Besides, in my experience, that solution seldom works for very long. Sooner or later you'll be dealing with holes with your new partner unless, of course, you can run like hell and never stop by taking drugs, smoking, or drinking a lot."

"That's not our style."

"So your next choice is to keep on doing exactly what you've been doing."

Dirk became irritated. "But what we've been doing isn't working!"

"True," the man said, his face lighting up, "But if you don't keep doing the things that you're used to, then you have only one option left. Some couples have opted for this last choice, but they are few and far between. That's because this is a terrifying choice for most people, and it requires a great deal of courage."

Dawn and Dirk winced. Seeing their reaction, the little man suggested that it might be best if he came back another time.

Recovering, Dirk begged him, "Please don't go! Tell us the last option."

"Are you really sure you want to hear it?"

"Yes! Yes! It can't be any worse than this," Dawn said, pointing at the hole.

"Believe me, you will consider it much worse. Whatever you think you have gone through before will seem miniscule compared to this choice."

"We're ready to try anything– just tell us what we have to do."

"Okay, but just remember, you insisted that I tell you."

"Agreed."

"Well then, the choice is to accept the hole."

This clearly was not the magical answer the couple had been hoping for. "But we've been doing that already," Dawn insisted. Like her husband, she was exasperated. "It seems like we've been putting up with this awful hole forever."

"I didn't say put up with it – I said accept it. You can allow the hole to become a part of you and your life."

The couple sat there dumbstruck for nearly a minute. What the little man was proposing seemed out of the question. Sensing their reluctance and unwillingness to trust him, he stood up and started to leave. The last thing he wanted to do was to push them when they weren't ready, but as before, Dirk and Dawn stopped him. Since nothing else had worked for them, they turned to him for guidance.

"What do we need to do to accept it?"

Sensing more receptivity the little man decided to share more with them, even though he knew they still would react to a lot of what he was going to say. "Well, there are two steps to take; one more frightening than the other."

Anxious to hear anything concrete after what they had gone through up till now, they verbally prodded him to tell them what they needed to do, regardless of their fears.

The little man continued. "You need to accept the hole as your friend and no longer judge it and treat it as the enemy. If you continue to regard it as the enemy you'll be running and hiding forever. You are then to watch and learn what happens when you do that."

Feeling somewhat cocky, Dirk asked, "Is that all we have to do?"

The little man warned them, "If that was so easy to do, you would have done it long ago, and remember that is only Step One. Very few people can even do this step. In fact, I can tell you that your ability to accept the hole and sustain it will, on many occasions, be fleeting and illusive. But I am certainly open to you calling out to me again if you need my help. You don't need to use the phone. I will hear you."

Regardless of his warnings, Dirk and Dawn made a strong commitment over the next month to treat the hole as a friend that they chose to accept despite their tendency in the past to see it as unacceptable. They made some significant strides in the way they looked at the hole and allowed it to be a positive part of their life. They even allowed themselves to move close to the hole, dangle their feet over the edge, look inside, and stop fighting with all of their uneasy feelings. As they did this they began to have a partial sense that the hole would adjust its size in relation to their level of acceptance. When they openly accepted it, it got smaller; when they started to reject and judge it, it got bigger. Even though they were still puzzled as to exactly how they could have such an influence on it with just their thoughts, there was no doubt that it was true for all to see.

For the first time they weren't trying to hide or get rid of the hole. And as they moved closer to one another in facing the vast emptiness, they began to experience moments of real peace and harmony.

Eventually, as they went back to their normal lives, their acceptance of the hole faded and they again found themselves reacting to it with fear and resentment. Frustratingly, they began to agree with the little man, that their ability to accept the hole was transient. Quite often they would start off accepting it, get frightened, and start judging it almost reflexively as they had done for so many years. Sometimes they would hear some judgment from others, not necessarily directed at them, and they would take it on as their own. It became a roller coaster of acceptance and rejection, with the hole changing in size with each momentary change in their behavior.

After many failed attempts to sustain their acceptance of the hole, they sought out the little man.

"How do we learn to develop a stronger acceptance," Dirk requested of him "Did you forget there are two steps?" the little man asked.

"I guess we did. Why didn't you tell us both steps at the same time?"

Lovingly, the little man stated, "I didn't think you could handle both, especially since you struggled with the first one, and this next step will make the first one seem like child's play. As you witnessed, the first step can only take you so far due to all your early training in the world, but you are to be commended because that is way beyond where most people go."

"What is the next step?" Dirk asked, becoming a little impatient.

"Before I tell you, I need to again warn you that you won't like hearing it and will probably call me outright crazy and reject it."

"Sounds like a place we have been before," Dawn anxiously joked with him.

"That's true, but you need to multiply it by ten."

With their curiosity overflowing, Dirk spoke. "Just tell us, okay!"

"Okay. You are going to need to join with the hole so that it becomes an integral part of who you are."

"Well, we barely understand what you just said, so how are we supposed to do it?"

"To be blunt, you'll need to let go of everything familiar to you and enter the hole," he said. "That is the only path to lasting peace, acceptance, and contentment."

Hearing this, they both gasped and trembled at the thought.

"Enter the hole? You've got to be kidding," Dirk exclaimed.

"No, I am not. I warned you that this would be difficult, but as I said, you don't have to do it. Most couples choose to reject this choice, but you can choose to follow their lead or not."

"It's just that we wouldn't be honest if we didn't tell you that doing such a thing scares us out of our minds," said Dawn.

"Being scared is not the problem," responded the little man. "I would think you were lying if you told me otherwise. The problem is being scared of being scared. The only question then that you need to consider is this: Are you willing to be scared? That is what separates the little boys from the men and the little girls from the women. Those who wait to not be scared are still waiting. The choice is yours."

Clutching each other's hands so tightly the blood could hardly flow, and their knuckles were turning white, Dirk managed to squeeze out the words, "Tell us more."

"While you will seemingly enter the one hole, it actually has several elements, and each one will expose you to different aspects of yourselves, which will serve you in moving through it toward your goal. However, all of the elements will threaten you in some way, just as the experience of the hole has threatened you from the very beginning. Whether you can get through these passages will rest on your willingness to surrender to all of the experiences. That is the key. So do we continue on this journey or do we get off here?" he asked them.

"Well, maybe," Dirk said hesitantly.

"Ambivalence will always be a NO," he replied, with no judgment intended. It's either two feet in or none at all is the way we play this game."

Sensing each other without even discussing it, they spoke simultaneously. "We've come this far; count us in."

CHAPTER FOUR ❧

INTO THE HOLE

Observing that they were now ready, the little man proceeded to explain the rules for entering the hole, which were very demanding.

"As I mentioned, the solution requires that you enter the hole. I will go with you, but most of the time in the hole you will not be able to see me; you will be able to hear me, but only at certain times."

Dirk knelt down beside the hole, and peered into its abysmal depths. He heard or maybe he just imagined the sound of subterranean winds whistling through distant caverns. The darkness invited them even as it threatened. What did it conceal? A labyrinthine maze? A devouring force? Dawn moved down beside him with her hand on his shoulder, as he voiced their anxiety.

"What if we go in and never come out?" That frightful thought was pounding so loudly inside their heads that they couldn't think of anything else.

"I hear you," the little man replied. "Of course you are afraid. Your fear is only natural and appropriate.

It is because you are going to be venturing where you've never been before."

Having become accustomed to the little man's usually brusque, matter-of-fact manner, Dirk and Dawn were pleasantly surprised by this new gentleness and understanding. They looked at each other, and Dawn nodded in response to Dirk's unvoiced question: Was she ready to make this descent with him and the little man? Yes, she was. Now having committed themselves, they were ready to be led.

"What do we hold on to?" Dirk asked.

"You don't," the little man patiently replied.

"Then, once we step into the hole we are going to be in a free fall without a parachute!" Dawn realized with shock.

"Hey, how about a parachute?" Dirk suggested hopefully.

The little man seemed amused. He smiled, shook his head and replied, "No parachutes. I believe it is called a 'leap of faith.' Do you have the courage to step into the hole and trust?"

The two young people contemplated the darkness before them, then looked at each other wondering if they were out of their minds to think of entering it.

"Can we put our lives into the hands of this strange little man?" Dawn whispered.

They made one more feeble attempt to bargain with him: "Isn't there an easier way down?" Dirk asked.

The little man just smiled and patiently explained, "You have a choice. You can live robotically as you try to protect your treasured images, hoping that you are never exposed, or you can become masters of your fears."

Dawn and Dirk thought about how their love was steadily dying because of their frustrating efforts to fill the hole. They realized there was little choice.

"Before you finally decide, I need to mention just one more thing for you to ponder."

"You mean there is something else? Isn't what you told us enough? We think it already sounds too difficult. We're not mountain climbers you know," Dirk blurted out.

"I hear your fear loud and clear. You need to appreciate that the hole represents a journey that you have never gone on, along with providing you with almost no familiar signs or signals," said the little man.

Not hearing anything new, Dirk remained annoyed that there would be so little to count on.

"It deserves repeating that once you enter the hole it will expose you to every part of your humanity and demand that you take a good look at these qualities. Many of these parts you've probably rejected and do not want to see, especially this clearly. The hole does not care about what you think is acceptable or unacceptable. To the hole it is all the same. You will feel like you are under a giant magnifying glass with every pore exposed."

"Haven't we already experienced these feelings?" Dirk questioned.

"You've experienced fighting against these feelings for the most part, nothing more. Also, once inside the hole, all the usual ways in which you typically deal with unacceptable things will be out of reach. Oh, and one more thing. There will be times in the hole that it will seem like you are on the edge of death, not just in a hole. This is because you will feel stripped of all the things that you identify with as YOU. You will not be able to hold on to the images you've cultivated or the feelings and thoughts that you've been attached to once you step inside the hole."

Dirk and Dawn were becoming even more terrified – if that was possible – with each new thing the little man imparted to them. Sensing this, he explained further. "I am not sharing this with you to scare you. I just want to make sure that you don't go in blind to what's involved here. This is not going to be easy.

"Boy that is reassuring. Do you have any other pep talks, Coach?" Without waiting for an answer, Dirk went on. "Well since I'm already scared silly, I guess it doesn't matter."

Dawn nodded in agreement and with that they walked hand in hand, if ever so slowly, closer to the edge of the massive, dark, empty hole, which, for all they could tell was bottomless.

"I'm terrified," Dawn said, her voice beginning to shake a little. "What if we never see our child again?"

As it happened, their child was staying with her grandmother for the weekend. Dawn could foresee the girl being raised by her grandmother instead of her parents, if they didn't return.

Visibly shaken, Dirk said, "At least she'll know that we took a risk to create a better life for her and that we did it together. We sure haven't given her much of a life the way we've been." After a brief pause, he took a deep breath and said, "OK, yes, we will go."

Regardless of their fear, they opened the gate surrounding the hole, and purposely not looking where the little man was, they jumped in, still holding hands.

CHAPTER FIVE ❧

THE LAND OF ETERNAL DARKNESS

Once inside the hole they were struck by the severe darkness, as Dawn and Dirk could hardly see a thing. When they jumped, they lost contact with one another. They desperately tried to reach out for each other, but in the end they grasped nothing. A terror unlike any they had ever known gripped both of them immediately. While each knew that the other was somewhere in the hole, being disconnected from the other was unbearable. Would they ever see each other again? Neither could imagine being without the other.

Dawn became ever more frantic. "Dirk, where are you?" she called.

Silence.

Dirk called out, "Dawn, where are you?"

Silence.

Suddenly they were each separately moving rapidly down what felt like a long, narrow slide. Their bodies appeared weightless as they were thrown around like feathers. The light from the surface of the hole began to get smaller and smaller with each passing moment until it finally totally disappeared from sight and they were in pitch darkness. The slides ultimately dropped them on to what seemed like a floor. Finally, being able to stand on something lessened their anxiety to some degree, but the overwhelming silence and the total darkness of the space left them feeling an increasing sense of panic. It seemed as if one hour turned into two, but with no way to determine time it could just as easily have been two days or two weeks. They feared that the darkness was all there would be forever, and their experience of the light above would just become a memory from their distant past.

Without realizing it, they began to each ask themselves the same questions. What if this is the end for us? What if we are doomed to never see or hear each other again? What if we never get to see the light of day again for the rest of our lives and will only know darkness forever? What if we are condemned to spend our lives merely wondering if darkness is all there will ever be?

Their fear of being consumed by the darkness occupied their every thought and feeling. The terror of these thoughts was unbearable, and created an obsession with finding some light somewhere. Several times in the hole they each thought they saw a flicker of light in the distance, but it turned out to be just a hope and a wish. Instead, the darkness remained ever-present. They each wondered where the little man was. Didn't he realize how much they needed him? With no sign of him their feelings intensified.

Very soon they began to feel that they were just blending into the hole itself, giving them each a sense that they were ceasing to exist. Dawn was not prepared to just submissively accept this, so she began to fight back.

"Stop this! Can somebody please stop this!" she shouted over and over again. In an intense and agitated voice she began to bargain with anyone who might be listening. "If you end this, I'll give you all that I own, or anything else that you want," she pleaded into the air. She kept ranting like this for what seemed like forever until her throat began to hurt.

Finally, annoyed by the continual piercing sounds, the little old man's voice came bouncing off the walls. "So you think you can bargain or shout your way out of here, do you?"

Feeling immensely relieved to hear him once again, Dawn said, "I didn't know you were here."

"I told you I would be here, but as usual you didn't trust me."

"But why did you abandon us for such a long time? We thought we were in this together and you were going to guide us. And now I don't even know where Dirk is!" she said frantically, on the verge of hysteria.

"We are in this together and I am guiding you."

"How can that be if you are not around? We are not experts in telepathy."

"But I am. There is no time that I am not aware of where you are and how you are doing. It's just that your minds are stuck on my being in some kind of physical form for you to know that I am there. As your guide, it is not always in your best interests for me to appear exactly the way you expect or exactly when you think you need me in order to assist you through this experience.

Right now, for you to go through the darkness you need to accept the unacceptable. Stop rejecting the darkness like you tend to do with most unacceptable things in your life, and embrace it."

"Well I'm trying and I bet Dirk is too."

"That's true, you are trying, but to go through it you need to appreciate what it actually means to go through an experience one hundred percent. A non-committal half-pie attempt, which is the most preferred style for human beings, just won't cut it. You've got to be fully committed and prepared to give all of yourself to this. The terror that you complain about is a sign that you are still holding on and not allowing yourselves to feel your vulnerability, which is being triggered by the darkness. Your minds are scaring you with all kinds of thoughts to get you to reject the darkness, such as the belief that you'll never see the light of day again. As a result your terror is prompting you to find a way to escape being present in the hole and it makes you deaf to hearing and being aware of your own senses. This is the way of most people. They see an experience coming, label it unacceptable, decide that it will involve pain, go around it, over it, or under it, but definitely not through it. It doesn't matter if it is fear, grief, or hate; as soon as you regard it as unacceptable, it's over."

"So how do we go through it?"

There was no answer as the little man's voice disappeared again, but in his place some strange things started to happen. All of a sudden the darkness was replaced by a bright light and the area they were in was totally lit up. They were thrilled to find that they could clearly see each other – and were closer than either had imagined. They rushed together and hugged each other for dear life. They quickly realized they could see every aspect of the hole. They felt safe again.

The hole appeared to be much bigger than they imagined and the grayish-blue walls were filled with small cave-like holes down both sides. One of the caves had a ten-foot triangle jutting out from it, which they realized they were standing on. All they saw above them was a long cone-like shape. Looking cautiously downward from the edge of their platform all they could see was a never-ending hole. It was overwhelming to be in such a large space and yet not a sound could be heard except for their shallow breathing. The air felt cool on their bodies and there was a funny musty odor present.

Then just as they were enjoying the light, it was gone. Once again they were enveloped in darkness. Instantaneously, they felt sad, disappointed, and afraid.

At the point where they felt hugely deflated, the room became totally lit again. And just as before, their joyous feelings returned and they were happy.

They began to hope that the darkness would never return and for these feelings to last forever. But their hope was disheartened when the darkness they feared appeared again and entirely consumed their existence. This pattern of darkness and light shifting occurred several more times, and their moods followed like a roller coaster.

The constant emotional changes soon made them feel that they were going crazy. In reaction to this turmoil Dawn screamed out once more, in the hope that the little man would hear her again. "We accepted the darkness like you asked, but we still like the light better."

"I know," was the immediate response. "But there are no favorites here like in your so-called every day world. You need to accept the darkness in the same way that you accept the light with neither being better than the other. "Are you serious?", they demanded. "Of course," the little man replied.

Dirk was surprised that the little man had replied, and let his frustration show. "We're not about to listen to any of this mumbo jumbo when our lives are clearly at stake," he stated. He encouraged Dawn to not buy into this and help him to find another way out of all this. But having no interest in Dirk's bravado at this point, she related that they need to listen to the old man's guidance especially since he had helped them get this far.

"We need to accept and embrace the darkness as he advised us," Dawn entreated.

"What does that mean? Why would we want to embrace something awful over something that we love?" he lamented.

"I'm not sure, but he's never tried to trick us before."

Dirk protested, "Doesn't he understand that we have to get rid of things in our life that are unacceptable or our life will be chaos?"

The little man's voice quickly confronted the two of them. "Where did you get the idea that rejecting and opposing something will ever get you anywhere? Whenever something is unpleasant in your life, you choose to expend great effort in opposing or rejecting it. Did you ever ask yourself if any of that really worked? I find it fascinating that you choose to jump into a dark, empty hole and you freak out as you discover it is dark. What did you expect it to be? You did the same thing when you first saw the hole, remember? You insisted on it being something other than a hole. Dark is dark, it is not light, but both are important in your life. Stop opposing the obvious and choosing sides. Learn to accept the unacceptable along with the acceptable. The old man witnessed the two of them struggle with this concept, but being in an exceptionally talkative mood he continued, "Think about it. To do otherwise is to declare war on the darkness in favor of lightness, as you have done so many times in your history. What impact can your willpower have when it faces darkness? You are not alone in this war, but it is a war you cannot ever really win. Do you really think that the empty darkness is going to get hurt, tired, angry, sad, or even react to your attempts to conquer it? Do you think that your empty hole is impressed with your numerous attempts to fill it, over the last few years? I hope this doesn't come as a surprise, but the hole was nothing more than amused. It didn't feel hurt or disturbed – it merely accepted all of your efforts. It just patiently waited until you were ready to accept the integrity of the hole and enter its dominion, as you now have."

Dirk and Dawn appreciated the little man's sharing all this, since they now realized they had gone so many years merely wandering in the dark having no idea what life was all about. Dawn began to see that throughout their life they depended on things being an unending series of acceptable pictures. With that realization she questioned Dirk.

"Are you aware how much we have avoided letting anything unacceptable into our life?"

"Well why would we want unpleasant things like sadness, fear and boredom to impinge on our wonderful existence?" he quickly responded.

Feeling more empowered Dawn challenged Dirk. "How developed are we really when something like a little hole can freak us out so easily?"

Despite not being used to her confronting him intellectually, he admitted, "You certainly have a point, but what would our life look like if we did allow in negative things?"

"I'm not sure, but there would be a lot less pressure." Feeling inspired by this exchange, Dawn found herself wanting more insights into the possibility of a different kind of life. She pressed the little man for more answers. Anxiously she demanded, "If we don't get to constantly choose to only have comfortable and pleasing experiences in our life, how do we deal with unacceptable feelings, like the incredible loneliness that the darkness seems to trigger in us?"

"You need to realize that your fear of your loneliness is merely a reflection that you are not at peace with being with yourself. You can't truly come together with Dirk until you get comfortable with your loneliness."

"But the loneliness is so painful," Dawn complained.

"Loneliness is not painful. The rejection of loneliness is painful. That is what creates the pain. Allow the loneliness and you will find that your pain is mostly an illusion. Loneliness," the little man said, "needs to be accepted in just the same way as the darkness."

But what he was saying seemed strange to them and definitely overwhelming. They found themselves becoming inexplicitly tired and just wanted to sleep. They dearly wished they could wake up in the morning to find that this had been nothing but a very bad dream. Having shut their eyes for what seemed like a very long time, they opened them suddenly. Dawn blurted out, "Where are we?"

Dirk, now wide awake, looked around and said, "We're where we were before, somewhere in a dark subterranean space. All I know is that it is still dark and I can't see a thing. I can barely make you out. Thank god I'm still holding your hand. It's my only security in the face of the darkness, except for the assurance from the little man that we need to trust the darkness more and stop rejecting it."

Still not quite ready to completely trust and accept the darkness, they continued to struggle for a way out of this dilemma. Dirk suddenly had a crazy idea, seemingly out of nowhere, which he knew they just had to try. He asked Dawn to follow his lead. Standing side by side, one pushed against the other's hand and with the other hand they each pressed against the side of one of the walls of the hole. In this stretched and somewhat awkward position the light again appeared and seemed to stay on, but there was no room to vary the intense leaning on each other. In an effort to keep the light on, they tried to stay in this position, but keeping their body and muscles tight proved to be very exhausting. Regardless, they made every attempt to hold the position out of their desire for maintaining the lightness. It was working, but they knew that their bodies would not be able to handle the strain much longer. With each moment they became more and more drained. This experience reminded them of the relentless pressure they felt when they were trying to cover up the ever-growing hole with whatever they could find. In that case too, there was no time to relax or ignore their unrelenting purpose. They wondered how many times people like themselves got into these situations for so-called legitimate concerns.

They heard the little man begin to laugh at what they were willing to put themselves through in an effort to stay away from the darkness, and ultimately ignore his teaching. He laughed even harder when they requested his help.

"It is comical that you ask for my help when I have already given it," his voice said, with a chuckle.

No longer able to keep up the pressure as their bodies were literally collapsing, in addition to the fatigue from their extreme emotional frustration, they let their muscles relax from the tension. As expected, the darkness immediately returned.

Exhausted, they decided to really listen to the little man and allow themselves to stop opposing the experience of the darkness and to accept whatever was occurring. They began to embrace and celebrate the lightness and the darkness without any objection. Fighting so hard against the depressive dread of darkness no longer seemed effective, and for the first time since they entered the hole they were able to feel lightness throughout their bodies. While they weren't sure if this would last, they didn't care. They were just thankful for the moment stemming from their acceptance of the lightness and the darkness, which they had previously considered incompatible.

CHAPTER SIX ⚜

A PLACE WITHOUT FORM

They felt at ease for what only seemed like a moment before the floor gave way and they were off sliding further down the hole at a fairly quick pace. After a while, and still holding hands, they began to speak.

"It feels like we have been traveling through this hole forever," Dawn whined. "Isn't there a shorter way?"

"Given that this is my first trip with you through an empty hole, I don't know what to tell you," Dirk replied. "I bet you think that I'm too stubborn to stop at a gas station and ask for directions for the shortest way. Or maybe we should go by AAA and get them to map it out?" Enjoying being facetious and also remembering some past trips they had gone on, Dirk burst out laughing. Dawn got a chuckle out of it as well but then went back to obsessing being on the road to nowhere.

"There's got to be a shortcut. For all we know, since we have been in the dark so much of the time, we might have passed by here before and not realized it."

"Could be," Dirk acknowledged, becoming more serious now. "It does feel like we are moving in an endless downward spiral. Before this hole came into our lives, it always seemed like we had a direction to follow."

"Maybe we just aren't any good at this," Dawn responded sadly. "Perhaps if we were smarter, quicker, or more powerful, we would be able to do better."

"Well, the little man didn't question us about our capabilities when he invited us to jump in. He only asked if we were willing to do it."

"Maybe he forgot to mention that there was a test we were supposed to take."

"Funny, but the little guy doesn't seem like the forgetting type."

No longer able to keep up the banter and maintain a sense of humor about their situation and provide each other with support, they both began to panic again as they felt totally lost. They found themselves feeling desperate for something familiar, something they could hold on to and relate to. In spite of their efforts, everything they counted on to help them organize their world, such as a job to go to or people to regularly see, was nowhere to be found in this empty chasm. They instinctively reached out for something to touch, waving their hands frantically, and they bumped into the sides of the hole. It was cold, damp, and very smooth, but they didn't care, as long as they could grab on to it. But there was nothing that they could grab on to; their hands just slipped off quickly. Every now and then they would discover a slight edge to cling to for a split second, but in the end the result was the same. Again they were detached from anything to ground them. Having no physical forms to rely on they tried falling back on their imaginations.

They began to think about their old world and how their identity counted on a variety of things to attach to. They internally visualized their house, car, child, friends, jobs, and TV programs among countless other things. When they weren't focused on things or people, they looked to their favorite images of pleasing and success that they loved. While they found momentary reassurance in this activity, without any reinforcement coming from their time in the hole it quickly became another hopeless venture.

In the end, left with nothing to identify with, they began to lose a sense of who they were. With no perspective of time it seemed like hours or even days passed, frequently without a sense of even the other person being there. They began to feel very disoriented.

After so much time without any stimulus to attach to, both Dawn and Dirk's world started to unconsciously get consumed with mostly terrifying images. At one point they imagined they were seeing what seemed like hundreds of bats coming straight at them and almost suffocating them. They felt that the bats would never stop coming, and then they were all gone leaving them with just the black emptiness.

Feeling desperate they screamed out again within minutes of each other for the little man to save them from this extreme discomfort. The little man responded rather quickly even though they had no sense of him during their struggle.

Dirk asked, "How do we hold on to a sense of who we are if we have nothing to identify with or attach to?"

"How can I know if I'm nice, if there is no one around to like me?" Dawn wailed.

"How can I prove myself," Dirk lamented, "when there is no one to validate me?"

"Sounds like your existence depends on something outside to support you," said the little man.

"Well, if there is no one to respect us, approve of us, or love us and we have nothing to care about, then who are we?" Dawn ask.

"Good question. In fact, it is a perfect question. What is your answer?"

They countered that they didn't know. "We only know that we are important if someone cares for us or we care about them. Without that we are nothing."

They found themselves extremely challenged when the little man stated, "Have you considered letting go of who you think you are?"

"Are you crazy?" Dirk shouted back. "What else is there but who we think we are? Without our identities we will cease to exist and will become nothing."

Without any means of defining themselves, they feared they would become mere blobs.

At this point they began to try all sorts of ways to convince the little man that they truly were the pleasing and perfect people they always thought they were. They drowned him in a stream of anecdotal evidence despite his suspected disinterest, but all their proof had the same impact as them trying to grasp on to the walls of the hole. Finally they became exhausted with their verbiage, but accepting his previous letting go statement seemed impossible to both of them, since they still dearly loved who they thought they were.

Regardless, the diminutive one went on. "Holding on to those images may help you to survive in the world beyond the hole, but in here we are only interested in the living, not people who are content with defending favored images that you both have spent your life maintaining. That won't impress anyone in here."

"Well, if I must say so, both of us were doing quite well in the world," Dirk countered. "Not only that, our belief in those images that you made light of was responsible for a great deal of our success."

Their defiant insistence on clinging to their perceived identities prompted the little man to repeat, "The only way to know who you are is to let go of who you think you are."

"I don't get it," Dawn griped. "How in the world can I let go of who I think I am and then miraculously know who I am?"

Sensing her sincere confusion, the little man explained. "It's paradoxical, but it is true. All the things that you hang on to for your identity, such as a high paying job, staying thin, pleasing others, or being intelligent, leave you in a dependent place. So when the job is gone, with it goes your identity. It's the same with the self-images that you each love. When no one validates that you are perfect, Dirk, you are lost. It's the same with you, Dawn, when your pleasing performance doesn't work. Only when you can let go of these images and the achievements that you are each attached to, can you have a sense who you really are: beings that are independent of all external things."

"What if we let go of all those images and we are left with nothing?"

"That is certainly your dilemma and poses a definite risk. While I would like you to trust what I am saying, I respect that you might not be ready to do that. My suggestion is that if at first you can't accept it, act as if you do."

"But what if…" they both began.

But before they could finish their question, the little man's voice was gone again and they were left to their own devices in the dark hole. Just as before, when they wanted to drown him with more questions, they could sense he had no interest in them using him in this way. His silence left them to ponder their own thoughts concerning who they really were.

Relying on his last words they decided to approach their fear about letting go of their identities. Dirk imagined that he wasn't perfect, and Dawn did the same with her people pleasing. But each time they tried, they were left feeling totally empty. They could only tolerate this feeling for a short time before they found themselves going back to their favorite identities. However, this time, instead of being content with their usual familiar images they once again proceeded to let go and allow themselves to experience the emptiness for longer and longer periods. As they expanded their capacity to feel their emptiness, they became less and less dependent on their usual narrow identities. The more they were able to support themselves in this way, the less their anxiety and agitation became, as well as their obsession with racing around searching to validate their favored images. For a moment there was calm …

CHAPTER SEVEN ⚘

THE DREAD OF POWERLESSNESS

Although they began to experience a new calmness in their bodies as a result of the last realization, the peace didn't last very long. Soon they found themselves again subject to an overwhelming anxiety triggered by familiar buttons. Being in an unfamiliar place, in the dark, lacking inner resources without external support, and exposed to forces beyond their control, they felt utterly powerless and vulnerable.

Exasperated and feeling victimized by their time in the hole, Dirk said to his wife, "Don't you hate feeling so powerless? All the ways that we used to count on to feel in control are gone."

"I totally agree with you," Dawn replied. "We used to think we had some power and control over our lives. Now it seems like that was merely an illusion, but at least it gave us some comfort. There is no time in the hole when I don't feel inadequate and powerless. Sometimes I feel like a walking limitation. That sure is very different from my life before we discovered the hole in our house.

"My, my," the little man's voice. "What a sad story. Well, the two of you have lost your way again. And I thought you were getting smarter about the game of life. I guess I was wrong."

Lacking any sense in the hole of where things ended or began, including themselves, they started to question what was actually real or unreal. Many times they assumed the hole was the same size as when they entered it: ten to fifteen feet across. But on this particular day some things started to feel different. They began to bump into the walls more often; there seemed to be less air; and the temperature seemed hotter. They wondered how this could be. The only answer that made any sense was that the hole was getting smaller. It seemed especially strange since most of their experiences in the hole had to do with it getting bigger.

When they lived in their home, they used to pray for the hole to get smaller, but now actually being in the hole, the idea that it was shrinking in size was not what they wanted at all! Yet it was quickly becoming apparent that it really was shrinking, and they could feel themselves being squeezed into a smaller and smaller space. Their fear of being crushed and facing death was becoming very intense and dominated their every thought.

Both of them braced themselves against one of the walls and put their feet against the other wall in the hope of stopping this danger. They remembered seeing a similar scene in some movie, but to be in it was definitely more terrifying. All of these attempts to stop the walls from closing in were just as futile as they had been in the past when they were trying to make the hole smaller at home. The same helplessness prevailed.

They couldn't understand that the little man would let things go this far. At other times he spoke up when their fear got this intense, but now he was not heard from at all. They questioned each other about what to do. Neither had an answer and their terror made it extremely difficult to think of anything clearly. With both walls flush up against their bodies, death seemed imminent. The empty hole was quickly becoming their coffin.

Finally, they heard the little man's voice, but all he said was, "So, are you going to accept and trust your powerlessness?"

"Trust powerlessness?" Dawn pondered. "Does he really mean that? He did say that."

"Of course, we are not going to just trust that. If we don't resist this, then our lives will be over," Dirk replied.

"Is it working?" countered the little man.

"Not yet, but we've got to keep trying to find a way to be powerful," Dirk declared.

"It's amazing to me how many times the two of you attempt to out-power situations you are confronted with even though it is not working," the little man said, shaking his head in exasperation. "In the beginning, when you first saw the hole, you attempted to cover it, then you chose to fill, hide, fight, and run from it. I guess you never heard of the saying 'whatever you resist persists'."

"We have, but we didn't realize it applied in such a dangerous situation as this," Dirk replied, defensively.

"Well then, be my guest and resist away," the little man scoffed, and the space between the walls got even smaller.

Seeing their faces turn red in an effort to stop the walls from shrinking further, the little man suggested they accept their powerlessness for just five seconds. Finally, having no alternative, they chose to listen, and to their disbelief the walls actually stopped moving. But, due to their inherent nature, they distrusted again and the space got tighter. They knew now what they had to do. Therefore, the next time they accepted their powerlessness for a longer period, the walls not only stopped collapsing but the area also became wider. They were thrilled that there was room for them to easily breathe again. As they accepted more and more, they no longer felt the threat of being crushed.

"How can this be?" Dawn questioned. "How can accepting being powerless make such a powerful difference?"

We never trusted in that way before," Dirk realized.

The little man could be heard whispering, "I wonder if you will the next time? I wonder if you will realize that only a truly strong person can stand up for his or her powerlessness."

While not fully understanding this, Dirk and Dawn, despite their uneasiness, were certainly more open to seeing powerlessness more as a friend and ally now – and for a moment all was quiet again.

CHAPTER EIGHT ⚭

"HOLEY" COMPLAINTS

For a period of time they contemplated all that had happened to them so far in the hole. Not being able to contain his displeasure for very long, as was his style, Dirk called out, "Hello little man! We have some complaints about this whole scene that we don't feel are being taken into account here. We realize that this isn't a four-star hotel, but even Motel 6 offers more than nothing. Are you there? Are we supposed to ring a bell to call? What are the rules here?" Dirk's impatient anxiety with the hole was really starting to blow his circuits and he began to rattle on endlessly. "I've read where people who go into space don't age, but I'm frightened that it is the reverse in this hole. Perhaps we are aging more quickly than usual, and if we ever get out of here, our child will still be the same age and we'll be eighty or ninety."

"Boy, that is one uplifting thought," exclaimed Dawn who was getting triggered by Dirk's discomfort. "Do you have any others?"

"Well ..."

"Stop! Don't answer me," Dawn cut in.

Pretending not to hear her, Dirk continued to obsess. "All this emptiness can't be good for your health. I don't recall going through the health food store and anyone recommending a bottle of emptiness. Yet, they seemed to have every other thing from tree bark to roots in all shapes and sizes – even wheat grass – but no empti- ness." He was really on a roll now. "And here we are be- ing fed a daily diet of emptiness with an ample portion of dullness. It is so dull in here that boredom seems excit- ing by comparison. I know! Why don't we start the first emptiness diet? Drink and eat emptiness and watch the weight fall off. People might get so scared of this diet, they'll be bingeing for days. Can you imagine the com- mercials for emptiness? Have a better life by bringing a little emptiness into it. You haven't tasted anything until you have tasted emptiness."

By now Dirk had completely depressed both of them with his unending monologue. Dawn finally got caught up with his soliloquy and chimed in with a chorus of her own displeasure. "Everything else, no matter how toxic, still amounts to something, and anything has to be bet- ter than nothing."

"Boy, the two of you sure make a lot of noise with those minds of yours. What's up now?" rang out the voice of the little man.

"We'd like to bring up some things we are struggling with and that we need you to take care of," Dirk de- manded in his typical do-things-my-way style.

"Sounds like you think we have a customer service department in here," answered the little man. "I'll listen, but I need to warn you that I probably won't satisfy you. So fire away. Who's first?"

"Do you want to start Dawn?"

"Well, don't you, Dirk?"

"But you had strong feelings."

"True, but so did you."

The little man raised his voice. "One of you had better start or I'm going to tune out."

"Okay, I'll go," Dirk stated. "We've been going through your endless obstacle course and we still don't know what is happening here or when this will end."

"Well, sounds like you're in a real dilemma because all the answers to what is happening lie within all of your experiences inside the hole, which is the place you are struggling to get out of."

"You are right about it being a place that we don't want to be. There are too many uncomfortable feelings here," Dirk responded.

"Of course, and that is your dilemma. You want to know what you don't know without going through the experience. You also want to object to everything and you think that will lead you to discovering answers. At this point you know that you don't know, which doesn't compute with your anxious minds."

Dirk always loved a debate and he wasn't going to back off of this one. "You call that knowing? I need to know when emptiness will become something and stop being nothing and what emptiness will become when it is no longer nothing."

The little man decided to play along with Dirk. "So you want to know something about nothing when you know nothing about nothing. You do realize that if nothing were something, it wouldn't be nothing."

"Now you are getting me all confused," said Dirk, with his head spinning.

"It's intended, but hopefully you know that."

"I'm really getting upset," he replied.

"With what? I thought you wanted to talk," said the little man.

"Yes we do; about all this emptiness."

"Emptiness is just emptiness. There's literally nothing in it to upset you."

"Well it makes me very sad," said Dawn.

"How can emptiness make you anything?" the little man countered.

"Easy. We feel lonely and abandoned."

"By emptiness?" he countered again.

"No, by what it does to me," Dawn replied, hoping he'd get it.

"Let me understand this. Nothing is picking on you and making you upset, sad, lonely, and abandoned."

"I don't know if it is picking on us, but it is sure making us feel that way."

"If nothing can do all that, I can hardly wait to hear what 'something' might inflict on you."

"Well I'm glad you brought that up ..." Dirk began, but stopped.

There was silence as the little man had tired of this circular talk.

"Where are you? You can't leave us now. I demand you answer us," Dirk continued.

Returning for the moment, the little man teased, "Dirkie, you seem to be getting all puffed up with yourself again."

"What's with the 'Dirkie' business?"

"I couldn't help myself since you were sounding like a little boy who is entitled to everything. You need to decide if you want to learn about what you have never learned before and which one of us is going to be the guide here. As always, I don't want to force anything on you. You are welcome to go back to your old life."

After a momentary pause, Dirk replied with uncharacteristic apology, "Sorry, I just got scared."

"I know," said the little man. "Most of the learning you are used to comes from the outside in; in that someone else or something is giving you knowledge. This kind of learning is limited to facts, figures, theories, and concepts. When you allow yourself to experience the void within you, you are learning from the inside out. Only in the latter way can you discover your deeper truths about love, passion, and spirit – the heart and soul upon which your life is based. Without learning this you will always be in disharmony with yourself, never fed, or feeling at home."

And with that the little man again withdrew into silence.

Undeterred by his silence, Dawn insisted on asking one more question that really puzzled Dirk and her. "You talk about the hole as if it can see, hear, and think for itself. Don't you realize that it is just an empty hole? It is not alive, like us."

The little man again broke his silence because he truly welcomed this question. I'm glad you picked up on that despite your enormous egos which say that life only exists in the form that you know. Haven't you noticed during your 'holey' war how responsive this seemingly lifeless hole is to your every mood, movement, and thought? Every time you have rejected the hole and tried to get rid of it, it grew bigger. On the other hand, when you accepted the hole and stopped fighting against it, the hole became smaller. Do you think that was magic?"

"We vaguely remember something like that happening when we sat at the edge of the hole in our living room, but I guess we mostly forgot about it as we struggled with our fears while actually in the hole. Being frantic with all that was going on we certainly hardly noticed it, and even then we thought it was just random," replied Dawn.

"In my eyes, it looks like a definite connection, but I guess the two of you fell back on your familiar beliefs and again thought it all just happened by accident. It can't be a game of chance when it always happens," the little man stated.

"Can you tell us more?" Dawn asked with thinly disguised desperation.

The little man sensed by now that they were using him to fill their emptiness so he chose not to reply and all their further requests fell on dead silence.

CHAPTER NINE ❧

THE BOTTOMLESS PIT

While holding hands was at times reassuring to them in the hole, it did not stop them from falling uncontrollably. Again they found themselves to be spiraling down to greater and greater depths within the hole, and again they tried desperately to find something to hold on to with no success. As a last resort they even tried to cling to related images and stories from the past in the hope that this would at least take them out of their fear of being in a hole with no bottom. This also appeared to be futile, but neither knew what else to count on to alter the floating anxiety that consumed them.

Dirk remembered having a similar feeling when he was eight years old and he was giving his first speech in front of a class. He was terrified. The paper he was reading from started to shake obviously and laughter began to fill the room. As hard as he tried, he just couldn't stop the shaking and everyone could see and hear the paper rattling. The humiliation he felt was unbearable and he was sure he would die of embarrassment. He was coming apart and there was nothing he could do. From that time on, he vowed that no one would ever see any weakness of his again.

At the same instant Dawn recalled being a little girl who lived with fairly aggressive, self-centered, and opinionated parents. She had gotten the message quite early that they were always going to be center stage and that there was no room for anyone's needs besides theirs. She learned that the only way to take care of herself was to please them, and they in turn would praise her for that.

She longed for a day when she could express her own thoughts and feelings without worrying about the approval of others. One day when she was seven, she took a risk and told them that she didn't agree with the way they made fun of her brother who happened to cry a lot. The disapproval on their faces was instantaneous, along with a lecture on their displeasure with what happened to their formerly good little girl. They stood over her and yelled that she was not to speak that way again. And she never did.

The terror of those experiences was, of course, magnified many times by being in the hole and feeling so unsafe. By now, both Dirk and Dawn were certainly aware that the little old man's initial warning was no smoking gun. Every situation they had gone though just verified his promise that every one of their fears would be revealed – especially their fear of anything unfamiliar. Even though it seemed like mere wishful thinking, they day-dreamed of a time when they would meet their final fear.

They began to notice that like so many of their other experiences, the more they rejected the falling, the faster they would fall. In those moments they would attempt to accept the sensations rather than object to them. And sure enough, the falling would slow down and there would be a momentary sense of calm. But the second they invested in holding on to the slowness rather than allowing it, the terror returned and they again started to fall at a rapid pace. They felt very frustrated that they still were not able to master their fear. Dirk suggested that they solve this accepting–resisting dilemma by wishing they would hit the bottom and crash so they could stop this endless freefall – presuming that there was an actual 'bottom' to this seemingly endless hole. Reluctantly they realized they were torn between the fear of letting themselves fall or the hopelessness of fighting it. They reminded each other how many times in their lives above ground that they would manipulate things so that they weren't caught in this dilemma. But the little man had already clearly stated that those ways wouldn't work in this hole. Regardless, they just kept repeating this pattern of falling and trying to stop.

Without even calling him, they finally heard the little man's voice mysteriously moving past them, going in the opposite direction.

"It sounds as if the two of you have fallen back into your hopeless, fearful, confused state, although there were moments in which you remembered some of your previous learning. How would you like me to help you?" he questioned.

"Can't you just stop us from falling and get us out of this terror?"

"I don't determine that; you do."

"When will that be?" they asked simultaneously.

"We've been at this forever," Dawn lamented.

"It is solely based on when you are ready to accept all experiences that life offers without your usual objections, guardedness, and preoccupation – and not just selective experiences either."

"Okay," said Dirk, "we will try to be more open and less reactive."

"Are you sure?"

"Yes we are."

"If you are really serious, then you need to totally surrender to the experience of falling into the emptiness. Only then will fullness be yours."

Dirk couldn't control himself and stated for what seemed like the millionth time, "You've got to be kidding."

Dawn immediately added, "What you are saying makes no sense. How in the world can emptiness become fullness? Everyone knows that emptiness is emptiness and fullness is fullness."

"Well, it sure didn't take long for the two of you to violate the commitment you made a second ago," replied the little man.

"Sorry," said Dirk, "but how in the world can we believe something so unbelievable?"

"Did it ever occur to the two of you that your devotion to your beliefs is the problem not the hole you find yourself in," stated the little old man. "All that happened from the very beginning was that I showed you an empty hole in your precious home. From that point on you both made up one story after another about the hole;

It's too dark, it's ugly, we hate it, it makes us powerless, it frightens us, and we can't live with it, to just name a few.

Dirk and Dawn countered, "Those aren't stories. All that really happened to us."

"Apparently the two of you cannot escape your conditioning, which has taught you the story that surrendering to emptiness means the end to everything you love, including your precious identities that you regard so dearly. In the world that you live in, surrendering is regarded as a dirty word. Even the thought of surrendering as you're falling into emptiness has not occurred to you, and the idea that it could lead to a positive experience would provoke further disbelief. But in a world that offers true peace and contentment, surrender is the *only* key that will unlock the door."

"Alright then, how do we surrender?" Dawn asked with great trepidation.

"It is not a *how*, it is a *risk*. You have all the skills you need to let yourself fall. What's missing is your willingness to be afraid, which is a definite risk. When you can allow yourselves to be afraid, you will be able to let go of all objections to falling."

Since they understood by now that arguing with the little man would lead them nowhere – and the fact that he had been right about everything so far – they needed to trust that completely surrendering and allowing themselves to fall within the empty space instead of fighting it was the only way out of their dilemma. So, with great hesitancy, they began to let go, feel the fear, and abandon all their resistance. They stopped trying to grab for the walls, flinging their arms wildly, dragging their feet wherever they could, holding their breath, and maintaining a mental stream of "no, no, no!"

Initially the terror enveloped them for what seemed like an eternity, but gradually, after many exchanges of encouraging words between the two of them, they began to rely on their trust in the little old man, which they had developed from their previous experiences. Finally, they gently held the other's hand and surrendered to falling into the seemingly bottomless pit of emptiness. Soon they released their hands and discovered that each moment they allowed themselves to fall and stop judging and fighting, they no longer regarded falling and emptiness as enemies and something to be feared. In fact, they were "becoming" the emptiness. What a strange sensation it was for them to actually "be" emptiness. They allowed themselves to join with all of the feelings contained within emptiness and really embrace it for what it was, and discovered, to their surprise, that it no longer seemed empty or frightening.

As they let go more and more, an odd feeling came over them and tears rolled down their faces – many tears for many fears. They suddenly realized how controlled their lives had been and the terribly destructive price they paid for the images and identities they were so attached to. They felt they no longer needed to maintain an image of any kind, especially pleasing or looking perfect. They had come to a place where they were free to be anything they wanted to be. It was a place where they had nothing to prove or defend. They could be as imperfect or displeasing as they felt. Who would have thought that there could be such a place? They now experienced a fullness they had never thought was possible.

A gentle smile was reflected on each face, and they instinctively reached out to hold the other's hand again, but not from their usual place of insecurity. Their days of running and hiding from the threat of the hole were over.

Amazingly at that moment it seemed as if they were no longer in the hole. Feeling disoriented from their long experience they weren't even sure where they were or how long they had actually been in it. All they really knew was that it was not dark anymore, and they recognized the little man standing there in front of them. It was the first time that they had actually seen him since they had entered the hole. There was an almost celestial light around him, and as he approached the brightness surrounded them as well.

The excitement they experienced as they stood in the light produced a heightened awareness and realization.

"We've all been duped," Dirk said. But not wanting to be a victim anymore, he rapidly revised this conclusion. "No, we'd really duped ourselves."

"Yes," said Dawn. "I see it now too. Here we had been running around searching for fullness everywhere and anywhere, hoping and wishing that the next experience, thing, person, would give us that elusive feeling. And each time, whatever we became attached to ended up being merely an illusion of fullness."

"Who would have thought we could discover fullness by surrendering to emptiness? Nothing could have been further from our minds," Dirk responded. "In fact, we wouldn't have considered such a thought even if we lived forever. In our conditioned minds where emptiness had been perceived as the ultimate enemy, it would never have occurred to us. If it weren't for that hole in our home, we would still be chasing around not understanding that we were way off the path."

"Do you recognize what truly happened when you accepted the experience of falling?" the little man asked. He wanted to make sure they fully appreciated their courage of accepting the necessity of letting go. "It happens many times with people that they successfully complete a task and then fail to appreciate it. They win a race, but soon after they are worried about the next race. Failing to appreciate their success results in them not fully completing an experience, and then they need to start the process in question all over again sometime in the future. It's a real waste."

"Yes, we are really learning to appreciate the wonder of acceptance. We also know that when we claimed to accept the hole before, we didn't fully realize all that was involved. However, now it is more than a word we say, it is part of who we are."

The little man smiled and said, "I love your realization because it shows that the two of you are really beginning to move beyond sleepwalking. Most people don't have a clue what acceptance really is. It is frequently associated with tolerance when the two are vastly different. Acceptance exists on four levels, all of which make up who you are as a human being: mental, emotional, physical, and spiritual. When you truly accept a part of you or some experience, you need to be able to say 'YES' on all four levels or you are still hesitating and avoiding what must be done. Of course, the more you fear something and have negative beliefs about it, the more difficult this will be. So when it comes down to accepting emptiness, nothingness and their relatives darkness, death, falling, powerlessness, dullness, or no attachment, you are entering the major league of acceptance. As I have stated throughout, you won't see many couples on this trip with you. There are no tour buses signing up to go inside a hole like this."

As this wonderful sense of fullness became their new reality, their being disoriented started to fade away. It became clear to them that they had returned to the living room in their house with the hole squarely in front of them. With that realization everything in their life took on a very different perspective. Resting from their exhausting trip by sitting in their love seat together, they gently looked at each other in what seemed almost like the first time. No longer were their eyes fixed on external appearances or the images they had been so attached to, such as proving their worth. Instead, they enjoyed the freedom and depth of merely loving the other for who they truly are … themselves.

CHAPTER TEN ❧

A "HOLY" FRIEND

That night, or at least they thought it was night, given that they had gotten used to constant darkness, they slept more soundly than they had in a long time. Toward morning they opened their eyes to see the little man standing by the side of their bed still watching their every move. He seemed intent on speaking with them.

"Within a short time you will never see me again," he said.

"Why can't you stay with us?" Dawn asked sadly.

"I appreciate your invitation, but I have other matters to attend to. Anyway you don't need me now."

"That's not true. We are more than likely to forget all this if you don't remind us."

"Well, you have a new friend in emptiness, so you don't need me now."

"We had certainly never thought of emptiness and nothing as friends before you invited us on this trip," Dirk remarked.

The little man reaffirmed their thought. "There is no better friend for you to have in the entire world. In having a friendship with emptiness and nothingness you have many wondrous gifts for you to carry with you for all time."

Affectionately challenging him, Dirk persisted. "Like what?"

The little man smiled. "Firstly, with this friendship you have little to be afraid of. After all, as you've seen, most of your fears relate to a concern that you will lose something. Well, if you are already comfortable with nothing, then loss is no issue, and no one can threaten you by saying that they are going to take something away. Secondly, closely related to the easing of your fear is the sense of freedom this friend offers you. You are free to move about in your world without having to look constantly over your shoulder for the dreaded emptiness that is going to catch up to you. Since you don't need to avoid this experience any longer, you are free to look forward to your heart's desire. Thirdly, you can, at last, feel secure knowing that whatever choices you make are truly yours and are not designed to simply protect you from the threat of emptiness as triggered by the loss of money, relationship, image, status, or possessions. Nor will you find yourself making decisions in your life to satisfy some underlying agenda, such as protecting you from feeling inadequate, insecure, or being disapproved of. Finally, since there is nothing to prove or defend, you can trust that whatever emerges out of the emptiness is your *truth*."

"Before you go, can I ask you if you think it is possible to share this with others?" Dawn questioned.

Dirk spoke up instead of the old man. "I don't think we can. They would just label us as some New Age psychobabblers. At best, our sharing with them would fall on disinterested ears or condescending minds. I can hear them now: 'Yes, we're glad the two of you had a nice experience. We're delighted we can come visit you more now. We'll be sure to join you some day on one of your holy trips,' they would say with a cynical glance at their partners."

Dawn, not being satisfied with Dirk's pessimism, turned toward the little man. "How do we get others to believe us?"

"You don't," he replied. "You are to live only your life knowing what real fullness is while being aware that the others have a hole, too. It is not your job to convince them of it or to persuade them to enter it. In time, they will discover their own."

"But that sounds too simple."

"It is simple. We just make things complicated due to our fears, and so the road becomes very difficult. Maybe now you'll understand why this journey is called 'the road less traveled.' If it were the road more traveled, you probably would've seen a much greater number of people in the hole than the small crowd that was actually there."

"Small crowd? We didn't see anyone."

"There are others, but it will take a while for you to make contact with them."

With that the little man turned around and vanished into the night air, even though they could hear him in the distance singing. Just faintly, they could make out the words of a song familiar to everyone; "He's got the whole world in his hands."

Their eyes welled up with tears at his departure, and they felt conflicted. While there was no doubt that they were going to miss him a great deal, they also felt blessed at having been able to know an individual like him in their lifetime. Their memories of him included some incredible experiences. Of even greater value, however, was that they had met someone so wise who always told them the direct truth, and whom they learned to trust on their dangerous journey. They were also reminded that he never betrayed that trust and in his way loved them throughout, although they didn't always realize it at the time. One doesn't come across mentors with that kind of integrity very often, if at all. Regardless, if they ever saw him again, they would never forget him. He was to be forever an essential part of who they had become.

CHAPTER ELEVEN ❦

MASTER OF THE HOLE

Walking outside their home, the bright sunlight enveloped them in a warm cocoon of security. They paused and stood on the front sidewalk feeling the wonder of the journey they had just completed. They kidded each other about the magic of being able to turn a hole into a whole. It seemed almost unbelievable that they could go from being victims of the empty hole to masters of it. They knew that being back in their home this time they would have a continuing respectful relationship with the hole and an understanding of its many messages and teachings. That knowledge was now part of their being and they would no longer be puzzled when the hole would change in size.

Ultimately they came to accept and welcome the hole as part of their home, even putting flowers around the edge of their new friend. However, whatever decorating they did, they would never deny the integrity of the empty hole. They even placed a sign next to it: Our Dearest Whole. Quite often they could be found sitting there with their daughter, feet dangled over the side, all of them holding hands and laughing out loud, as they shared with each other the many stories involving their time with the hole.

EPILOGUE ⚶

In ending this story it is important to note that this is a fable, not a fantasy, so it is not the intent to say that Dirk and Dawn lived happily ever after. Just as they had predicted on the morning they stood in front of their house, there were numerous occasions when, due to various reasons and certain circumstances, they lost an awareness of what they had learned from the hole. This forced them to slip back and unconsciously reject their emptiness. But now being masters of the hole, they were fairly quickly able to regroup and reconnect to their essential purpose of living and no longer merely surviving in a world of forms and images. From this perspective they could choose to again join and embrace their "holy" friend, while laughing at themselves for taking themselves too seriously.

Our couple came to understand that while they might never find out what was really happening in their neighbors' homes, it no longer mattered. They knew that all the others had a hole also, but that they would reveal it only when they dared to take a similar journey.

Thanks to the courage of Dirk and Dawn the secrets that I mentioned in the beginning have been revealed to you. Now the choice is yours as to whether you go through this door to find the peace that is rightfully there for you. Always remember that life is a series of doors with various unacceptable parts of your character to be challenged behind each one. Your decision to accept these challenges will not only determine whether your life will be a struggle or a loving adventure, but also whether it will be one of openness to live in the present rather than one of regret of the past and dread of the future.

ABOUT THE AUTHOR ✎

Bruce Derman, Ph.D. is a licensed clinical psychologist who has been in private practice as a psychotherapist for over 40 years in Woodland Hills and Santa Monica, California. He specializes in high conflict couples, sexual and eating disorders, and divorce mediation and coaching. He has written two other books entitled "We'd Have a Great Relationship, If It Weren't For You" and "We Could've Had a Great Date, If It Weren't For You". Dr. Derman works with many people in his private practice who are struggling with the issue of emptiness in their everyday lives as a result of exposure to different losses. He helps them to move through this dilemma so that they can learn to accept their emptiness as a natural part of their life's journey. He can be reached through his website: therelationshipdoctor.net or via his email: relationdr@aol.com.

To purchase additional copies of "The Hole", please remit $11.95 plus $3.00 for S&H to Dr. Bruce Derman, 23011 Oxnard Street, Woodland Hills, CA 91367.